THE VACATION

A ROOM FOR 3 SHORT STORY

ANA ASHLEY

COPYRIGHT

products of the author's imagination or used in a fictitious manner. Any resemblance to actual persons, living or dead, or actual events is purely coincidental.

COVER DESIGN: Rhys, Ethereal Designs

Editor: Abbie Nicole

Join Ana's Facebook Group Café RoMMance for exclusive content, and to learn more about her latest books at www.anawritesmm.com!

CONNECT WITH ANA

Connect with Ana on social media:

Hang out in my FB Group Café RoMMance
Follow me on Instagram
Follow me on Bookbub
Sign up to my newsletter
Become a member of Ana's Attic

CHECK out more of Ana's books:

Dads of Stillwater series
Chester Falls series
Room for 3 series
Finding You series
Christmas Bubble
Midnight Ash
Stronghold

And for an overview of all my books and audiobooks, visit my website!

DEDICATION

THERE'S nothing like a semi-forced break to help replenish the creative well.

Having my family visiting recently was the perfect excuse for a much-needed vacation.

As soon as they left I started writing The Vacation. The story flew out of my fingers as if it was destined to be written.

It's short. It's sweet. It's a little sexy.

It's everything you can expect from Ana Ashley.

So for all the creative minds out there? Don't be afraid to hit pause.

BLURB

Three men.
One cottage on the beach.
A life changing vacation.

Felix

I'm in love with my two best friends...the problem is they can't stand each other.

But I have a plan...one that could blow-up in my face.

Everett and **Grayson** didn't always hate each other. In fact, the way they looked at each other I'd put my money on the opposite. But then something happened and everything changed.

Now with both men under the same roof will this be the perfect chance for them to kiss and make up? And in the battle for the biggest bed, which one will have room for three?

The Vacation is a standalone contemporary MMM romance that features three men who can't help falling in love in the close proximity of a beach cottage. This is a short story in the Room for 3 series.

1

EVERETT

I LEANED against the wall as if I could merge to it and closed my eyes, trying to keep my breathing steady. There was a one thousand percent chance the rail next to the stairs leading to the ferry's upper deck had never been gripped so hard before.

"Have this. It'll make you feel better," Felix, my soon-to-be-former best friend, said, handing me a bottle of soda.

"I'm not seasick."

"You look a little green though."

"I don't like boats," I lied but took the bottle and downed half of it.

He looked so guilty I almost felt sorry for him... almost. But he'd brought me to my own personal nightmare, so I was going to let him stew on it, at least until my feet were safely back on land.

"This isn't a boat, Ev. It's a ferry. And have you seen the size of it?"

"I've seen enough. How long is it until we get to the island?"

We'd flown from New York to LA, where I thought we were staying. When the cab from the airport stopped at the ferry terminal to La Catarina island, I was ready to turn back and go home, but Felix's pleading green eyes made me cross the bridge of death onto the ferry.

"Not long. I can see land already, so maybe another ten minutes?" he said.

"What's so special about this place anyway?"

"You'll see."

I looked at him and couldn't help smiling. Felix had been trying to get me out of the city for months, but it had been a difficult few months for my business, so I'd put it off until I ran out of excuses.

Even though I had agreed to come on this short break, I still felt guilty for leaving my custom print store in the hands of my staff.

It was only for a few days, and considering the store would be closed over the weekend, I really couldn't argue that it wouldn't survive without me.

I felt like I took my first breath in hours when my feet hit solid ground. The ferry terminal was small but busy as people waited to get on for its return to the mainland.

Breathing the salty sea air, I couldn't deny I was already feeling a lot more relaxed. I just hoped getting to the resort didn't require the use of another floating device.

"Come on, it's this way. We can walk there," he said.

The resort wasn't far, and because we were only staying a few days, I hadn't bothered with a big suitcase. Felix, on the other hand, was struggling to pull his huge suitcase over the cobbled path once we crossed the gate toward the main building.

"What have you got in there? A body? Are you trying to smuggle someone in?" I teased.

"Funny. I just want to be prepared for any eventuality. You never know what might happen."

I looked at him. "Are you hoping to hook up with someone?"

Voicing my thoughts left a strange taste in my mouth. Felix was single, so technically, he was free to hook up with anyone he wanted. Just because I had a small crush on my friend, it didn't mean I would stop him from having fun.

Besides, he'd already reassured me we'd have separate rooms. Even though our last vacation together was a few years ago, having to share a bed with him for three nights was still up there in my list of personal nightmares.

Okay, so sleeping with Felix in the same bed wasn't quite the same as going on a boat. There was no way I'd ever get an erection on a boat. More like my dick would recede deep into my body in reaction to the fear.

"Um…no. I mean, if it happens…it happens," he said. The hope in his voice was my realization that my idea to bring my e-reader with me was a good one. I could always keep myself busy reading if I ended up on my own.

The main resort building was modern and looked like it had been through recent renovations. The marble floor spoke of money while the inviting couches in the lounge by reception looked comfortable and luxurious.

"Good afternoon and welcome to the Silver Sands Resort. My name is Betty. I take it you're here to check-in."

The reception desk girl had a big smile like she genuinely enjoyed her job.

"Yes, please," Felix said. He'd been the one to book the vacation for us, so I looked around the large lobby and the garden beyond the wide glass doors while he checked us in.

There weren't as many guests around as I'd

expected. Felix was a teacher, so we had to wait for his fall break to take our vacation. Fortunately, his school broke earlier than some, so we'd caught the end of summer rather than the beginning of fall. And we were off the coast of LA, so there was that.

"Okay, I've set you up with three keys, and Marco will take you to your cottage," Betty said.

I turned back to the reception desk.

Three keys?

"Felix?"

He took the cards from Betty, who informed us we could still catch lunch in the main restaurant, but he didn't acknowledge me.

"Felix," I said again.

"Let's follow Marco with the luggage so we can get our bearings first, okay?"

I pursed my lips but did as he asked. There was no point in standing in the lobby asking questions.

The cottage was beautiful. It had an open-plan kitchen and living room with a fireplace as you walked in. I could see how it would be a great place for a late fall or winter vacation too.

Beyond the lounge was a corridor leading to the bedrooms, and upon further investigation, the suspicion I'd had at reception was confirmed. Because from where I stood, unless the cottage had an office, library, game room, or anything else as random, there were three bedrooms.

"You're all set, sir. You can call the reception desk any time if you need anything. There's a small folder on the table with information about the resort, including activities you can participate in and rules about feeding the bunnies," Marco said before he left us.

When Felix's eyes met mine, I knew something was up.

"Spill it. Who else is coming? And for your sake, you better not say Grayson," I said, crossing my arms.

He shrugged apologetically. "It's Gray."

2

GRAYSON

"Can I get you anything to drink, Mr. Davenport?" the flight attendant asked.

"No, thank you. I'm good. How long until we land?"

"One hour, sir."

"Thank you."

I moved my focus back to my laptop. I could do another thirty minutes of work before I shut it down for the next few days. My assistant could always get hold of me on my phone, but I was hoping to be left alone one last time before my life changed.

A ping sounded, so I turned down the volume and opened the private messaging app everyone in the company used, from CEO to mailroom assistant.

Fuck, just what I needed right now.

. . .

Robert Davenport: Good afternoon, Grayson. I went to see you in your office, but your assistant told me you left early.

Grayson Davenport: Hi, Dad. I had a flight to catch. I'm away for the next few days, remember?

Robert Davenport: So you finally decided to listen to your father and meet with the Coulsons? I hear Aspen at this time of year is rather nice.

Grayson Davenport: No, I'm on my way to LA to spend some time with Felix.

The back of my eyes started hurting. I hoped I didn't get a migraine. It was all I needed when I was desperate for some time away from the corporate world and especially my family.

Robert Davenport: Felix? Son, you need to spend your free time making connections. Networking. You're only a few weeks away from being CEO of one of the most successful corporations in New York. The press will have a field day if you're caught behaving like you did in college.

Migraine successfully installed.

. . .

Grayson Davenport: The definition of free time is that I can do whatever I want with it, Dad. I network and make plenty of connections while I'm at work. Hence why I haven't seen Felix for months.

Robert Davenport: Just stay out of the press. I suppose you can come back refreshed and ready to step into your new shoes.

I groaned and closed the laptop. There was no way I'd get any work done now, so I took a couple of Advil and closed my eyes, hoping my head would feel clearer by the time I landed at LAX.

Felix had definitely outdone himself with the choice of location if the website for the Silver Sands Resort was anything to go by.

I was certainly looking forward to their water-based activities. Maybe I could even convince Felix to try them with me.

Most times, you could take the teacher out of school, but you couldn't take the school out of the teacher, which meant I was constantly on the wrong side of a safety lecture.

God, I missed Felix. Why had I gone so long without seeing him?

Oh yeah, because I was about to take over my dad's company before he retired. Because I'd been required to attend dozens of social events so everyone started accepting me as the face of the Davenport Corporation.

I checked my personal email for an update from Felix. Of course the thorough Mr. Davis had detailed instructions on where to go once I arrived at the island.

He'd added a selfie, which he'd taken in the bedroom of his Brooklyn apartment. Behind him was a suitcase filled to the brim with clothes and shoes, but what I couldn't take my eyes off of were Felix's happy green eyes.

Was it selfish to want to get lost in them? To want more from Felix than friendship when I knew I was about to lose the little freedom I had?

Yes, it was, and it wouldn't be fair to him either. Not that he'd ever want more from me. We'd had plenty of chances to take things further, and he'd never indicated that he was interested.

His world seemed to revolve around his job as a teacher and Everett.

Ugh, Everett. The frustrating if sexy as fuck other best friend of my best friend.

Not that I had a problem with him. He was the one that seemed to have a problem with me.

Okay, so maybe I shouldn't have come on to him and offered to fuck his frustrations out two Christmases ago.

My dick thickened as I remembered the scent of his aftershave. I'd been beyond drunk, but I still remembered every detail of Everett's plump lips, wet from his drink. The way he clung to me on the balcony of Felix's apartment as if he'd die if he let go. The way his blue eyes looked at me as if he were seeing me for the first time, even though we'd known each other for years through Felix.

Of course that was before he kneed me in the balls, called me some choice names, and left me standing in the freezing cold trying to catch my breath and get sensation back to my groin.

As the plane started its descent into LA, I shook off thoughts of Everett. The next few days were all about Felix and me.

Even if I couldn't get what I wanted from him, I could make sure we both had enough fun to last us a while.

3

FELIX

FOR THE THIRD time in the last couple of hours, I knocked on the door of the bedroom Everett had claimed for himself. Still no answer.

"Come on, Ev. You can't stay mad at me forever. Plus, I have food," I said, hoping to draw him out.

I knew this was a long shot, and there was a chance both my friends would stop speaking to me for some time.

One down. One to go.

Gray had texted to say he'd landed and was taking a cab to the ferry terminal.

When he'd said he was taking a later flight due to work, I didn't argue because if Ev and Gray knew what I had planned, they'd never leave JFK, let alone come on this vacation.

Not that I'd tell them the reason they were both

here anyway. With some luck, they'd work through whatever shit they had going on between them and become friends again, like they'd been when I'd first introduced them a few years ago.

If I was lucky, things would…hell, what was I thinking? There was no way things would ever go the way I wanted them to go.

Ev unlocked the door but didn't open it. There it was, my invitation to make things right.

I ran back to the small kitchen, put some food on a plate, and grabbed a bottle of water. A moment later, I opened the door, bearing my olive branch of food offerings.

"Hey," I said.

Ev was sitting on the chair facing the floor-to-ceiling glass door that led to the garden. The room didn't have a beach view, but it wasn't any less beautiful.

"Why didn't you tell me?" he asked.

"Because I knew you wouldn't have come. Neither of you would."

"Does he know?"

"No."

He looked at me with wide eyes.

"He's going to think this is a setup."

I sighed.

"This *is* a setup. I'm so sorry, Ev. I'll explain everything to him, I swear."

He took the plate from me and started eating like he hadn't for days. I knew that would work for Ev. The way to his heart or out of trouble was definitely through his stomach.

"You better have some cake hiding somewhere too," he said, still chewing his food.

"It's in the fridge," I chuckled.

We sat in silence while he ate.

Ev had taken the last bedroom in the corridor, which left me with the middle one to avoid them being too close to each other.

Not that I minded being in the middle of them both. No. I actually craved it as much as my next breath. But how did I explain to my two best friends that I wanted more from them? Not just for myself, but for each other.

I wanted them to see what I could see. They were perfect. Funny, engaging, hardworking, and so fucking good-looking neither should be allowed outside around lowly average-looking humans.

"So what are we doing while we're here? Thank fuck, he'll probably be busy trying to get killed by hanging from a rope or diving from a cliff, so it's unlikely I'll see him much," Ev muttered.

I couldn't help hoping he was as worried about

Gray's love for adrenaline as I was, and for exactly the same reasons.

When he finished his food, he put the plate on the nightstand and sat on his bed with his legs open and back against the headboard.

As always, I took my place against him, feeling my heart beat extra fast as he wrapped his arms around me. There was a height difference between us, and since I was shorter and smaller, it felt natural to cuddle up to Ev this way.

"I'm sorry. I don't want to bring the mood down," he said in my ear. "I'm sure Gray and I can put up with each other long enough to make this a nice relaxing vacation for the three of us, right?"

"Right." I leaned my head back on his shoulders, my brain imagining Ev turning his face and kissing my neck all the way to my ear lobe.

It would never happen, but a guy could dream, right?

Next thing I knew a bell rang, and I opened my eyes.

What the…? I must have fallen asleep in Ev's arms because I was still in the same position I last remembered.

Short puffs of breath tickled my neck, so I turned my face a little and saw Ev had also fallen asleep. I watched him for a second, admiring him from close up.

What wouldn't I do to have this every day?

The bell rang again, waking Ev up, and suddenly, our eyes locked. I'd been caught staring.

"I um…bell…I think Gray is here," I mumbled.

Ev didn't move for a few seconds. His eyes bored into mine as if he wanted to be like this a little longer before he released me.

I left the room and was surprised to see Ev following me to the door.

Well, at least we'd get the hard part over sooner rather than later. And if Gray had the same reaction Ev did, there was still plenty of food left in the fridge, thanks to the super helpful waiter that served me when I'd walked into the main restaurant, hoping they also did takeout.

I took a deep breath and opened the door.

Before I could let it out, I was scooped up in Gray's embrace. My feet hung off the floor, and I had no choice but to wrap my arms around his shoulders.

Gray was as tall as Ev but not as built. Not that he was any less strong, as evidenced by how easy he could pick me up.

"I hope there's food here because I'm starving," he said.

"There is."

"And cake," he followed like I knew he could.

"The cake is all mine, so you can go get your own if you want some." Gray froze at Ev's words and put me down.

He looked into my eyes. "Am I hearing voices or was that Mr. I-Have-A-Stick-Up-My-Ass that just spoke?"

I groaned.

"I can assure you there is nothing up my ass, not that it's any of your business," Ev said.

Jesus, this was going to end in a fistfight.

Gray quirked his head, still not letting go of me. "Maybe you do need something up your ass to help you chill a little. I know a guy."

Ev turned around and headed toward his bedroom.

Gray looked at me, finally letting me go. "What the fuck, Felix? You could have warned a guy."

I shrugged. "Ev is here. Surprise."

4

EVERETT

"Okay, I'll give it to you. You made an excellent choice with this place," I said to Felix, who was lying on the lounge chair next to mine, his eyes closed as he took in the warm sun.

He turned his face to me. "It's nice, isn't it?"

I nodded. The resort had its own private beach, and our side seemed to be populated mostly with guests from other cottages.

"What are you reading?" he asked, pointing to my e-reader.

"*Tough Love* by Griffin Prescott."

He sat up on the lounge chair. "I love that book so much. You have to finish it so we can talk about it. Griffin is such a talented author."

"Right? I love his writing."

Felix leaned over like he was going to tell me a secret. "Did you know he lives on the island?"

My heart rate and curiosity spiked. Surely he didn't mean that my all-time favorite author lived right here, probably within a few miles from where we stood.

Felix nodded, his smile wide and warm.

"Do you think we'd spot him if we went for a walk outside the resort?" I asked.

"We might be lucky enough to see him here. Did you know his husband runs this place?"

"Nooo…"

Felix laughed. "I was joking. He probably doesn't, but wouldn't it be cool to run into him?"

"Run into who?" Grayson asked, sitting next to Felix. He was dripping wet from the sea, and I had to admit, he looked good enough to eat in his swimsuit.

Grayson was lean but had muscles in all the right places, and that fucking stupid V leading to what was likely an amazing cock, should be illegal. I'd never seen it, but considering the damn man was all but perfection, it wouldn't surprise me if he also had a nice thick, long dick. The fucker.

He coughed. "Like what you see?"

Fuck.

"I was just thinking how inconsiderate of you to get Felix's lounge chair soaking wet. Rude much?"

Smooth, Everett, very smooth.

I raised my e-reader to continue with my book.

"Felix doesn't mind. Unlike some people, he's actually chill, and he likes me," Gray said.

"*Some people* are plenty chill. But you're right. They don't like you," I replied. "I'm going for a walk."

I stood up and locked my e-reader before tucking it under the towel. Then I walked toward the water, where the packed, wet sand was easier to walk on.

Once upon a time, I considered Grayson a friend. We weren't as close as I was with Felix, but we got on well enough until the Christmas party two years ago.

When I had some distance, I looked behind toward the lounge chairs. Felix's gaze was focused on Grayson and whatever he was saying. He seemed genuinely happy.

I continued walking, letting the water only touch my feet as it came and went on the beach.

I'd always suspected that Felix had a crush on Grayson, but I was pretty sure nothing had ever happened between them. What I couldn't understand was why he'd invited me along when he could have had Grayson all to himself for a few days.

Grayson had always been a touchy-feely guy, so there was a good chance he wouldn't mind taking things further with Felix.

Why did the thought of the two of them together

not make me jealous? Maybe it was because I wanted my friend to be happy. Yes, that must be it.

"Hey, Ev. Wait up."

I turned to see Felix running toward me. When he caught up, I kept walking but moved so he was on the side near the water. He narrowed his brows but didn't say anything.

"Why don't you like Gray?" he asked.

"What? I don't dislike him. He just…frustrates me."

"From where I stand, it looks a lot like you don't like him. Hell, you even said it not ten minutes ago. I want to know why."

I took a deep breath, taking in the salty sea air. What could I tell him? Definitely not the truth.

"I said it to him because he's a cocky bastard who thinks he can get whatever he wants. It's not… it's not how I really feel. You know me, Felix. Unlike what Grayson says, I'm not really stuck up and stiff."

He raised a brow and eyed my shorts.

I laughed.

"Eyes off, you pervert," I said, bumping my shoulder with his.

"Seriously though. I'm friends with both of you," he said. "I'd love it if you could get along. I barely see either of you as it is."

I stopped and turned to face Felix. The lightness I'd seen earlier was replaced with sadness.

"Hey, come here." I pulled him into my arms, and he came as he always did.

Felix was absolutely the right height for me. How could I not have feelings for him when even physically, we fit so perfectly together?

He relaxed under my touch, but I could feel there was something more bothering him.

Was I ready to hear him admit his feelings for Grayson? Was that why he wanted us to get along? It made sense. If his best friend and boyfriend got along, it would make his life a lot easier.

"I promise I'll make an effort with him, okay?" I said.

He nodded and then stepped away from my embrace.

We walked a little further up the beach until he stopped in his tracks.

"What's up?" I asked.

"Look! That's Griffin Prescott, holding hands with that guy."

I gasped. "Shit, we saw Griffin Prescott in person. This is already the best vacation ever."

"Do you think that's his husband?" he asked.

"Don't know. He doesn't really share photos of him on his social media, which I totally get now. The guy is stunning." They seemed to be around the same age, which was weird because I always got the vibe that Griffin's husband was older whenever he mentioned him on his social media.

"Shall we walk back before we're arrested for salivating over a local celebrity?" Felix asked.

I chuckled and put my arm around his shoulder. "Let's."

5

GRAYSON

I LOOKED up from Everett's e-reader and saw they were both walking back, so I locked it and put it back where he'd placed it under his towel.

He'd be pissed when he realized not only had I been reading his book, I'd also bookmarked where I stopped, but not where he'd stopped.

The thought made me smile.

Why did I like to rile up Everett James so much? That was one of the greatest mysteries of all time.

Everett and Felix were wrapped up in conversation, so I took the chance to observe them. Sitting in board meetings was mostly about reading body language, so I'd gotten pretty good at reading the signs people didn't want me to catch.

And I was catching it all right. There was no question that Felix had feelings beyond friendship for

Everett, and from the way Everett looked at Felix, they seemed reciprocated.

I hadn't seen Felix for a while and Everett even longer. Had they hooked up since?

Felix would have told me, wouldn't he?

The thought sat heavy in my stomach, and staring at both of them as they got closer, I wasn't sure who I was jealous of.

Sure, I had feelings for Felix. I'd had them for a long time. But Everett? Nah…I didn't. Not a chance. The man was so stuck up I wasn't sure anything would ever get through to him.

Except he hadn't always been like that.

"I'm going to head inside for a shower. I'd like to explore the town before we go to dinner."

Felix's words brought me out of my thoughts, and I only just nodded in time to see him walk past toward the cottage.

Everett stared at me for a moment. I waited to see if he was going to say something, but he didn't. He came around to his lounge chair and picked up his towel and e-reader.

He looked at it and then at me. "You read my book?"

"It's a good book. I didn't know you liked sexy stories. Maybe you're not as frigid as I thought." Yep, I was really asking for it.

If his eyes could shoot daggers, I'd be sliced into tiny pieces by now.

"Why would you do that? You didn't even bookmark—" He let out a growl and then came at me, except I'd put sunblock on recently, and my skin was slippery, which meant he fell forward onto the lounge chair.

My reflexes worked before I could make sense of what was happening and held on to his waist, but he was too heavy, and since I'd been sitting on the edge of the lounge chair, we ended up on the sand.

Well, I ended up in the sand. Mr. Everett James ended up on top of me.

And because my brain really wasn't working properly today, the first thing I thought was how good he felt. But then my mouth had to go ruin it.

"If you wanted to pin me down and take me, you could have just asked, you know?"

"Fuck you, Grayson."

"What, while everyone's watching? I never thought you had it in you, baby."

His large blue eyes bored into mine, and I had to think about contracts so I wouldn't get hard. I wasn't sure he realized that he really was pinning me down with his large hands, and there was nothing but two soft and thin pieces of cloth between our dicks.

"Why are you like this?" he spewed but didn't move an inch.

"Like what?"

"You joke about everything. You don't respect anyone. Has your privileged life made you forget that people are human and have feelings?"

That did it for me. I used my strength to push him back, and he clearly wasn't expecting it because he fell back on the sand.

I stood up and brushed the sand off. "You don't know anything about me or my so-called privileged life. Have you ever heard the expression, don't *judge someone until you've walked a mile in their shoes or a day in their life?*"

He let out a long breath. "I'm sorry, okay? I didn't mean that. Can we just...can we keep it civil for Felix's sake? He's hurting because of us, and it's not fair after he worked so hard to bring us all here."

His comment hurt more than it should have. I'd been hearing similar things since the day I was born, and I usually had a smart answer for them. But somehow, having it come from Everett cut deep.

He was right though. Felix didn't deserve this.

"Okay. I'm sure we can do that. And I'm sorry I read your book. If it helps, you were on location 2530."

He stared at me and then picked up the e-reader.

A moment later, he looked up with his mouth open. "You memorized it?"

"Unlike popular belief, I'm not actually a dickhead."

He raised his brows, and I smiled.

"Okay, I'm not *always* a dickhead."

"That's better."

The tension between us disappeared, and there was no longer anger in Everett's eyes. Maybe something else I couldn't read, but at least it wasn't anger. I could work with that.

"Come on, for that stunt, dinner's on you," he said, walking toward the cottage.

"This is an all-inclusive place," I said, laughing.

"Not for the drinks."

6

FELIX

Maybe they ate magic mushrooms.

Or an alien life form kidnapped them and brain-washed them before returning them to earth.

Whatever happened after I left to have my shower must have worked because Ev and Gray were acting normal. Well, as normal as they could act, which usually wasn't very normal at all.

Still, I hadn't had to stop Gray from jumping off a cliff or remind Ev that his shop wasn't flooding or collapsing while he was away. That was progress.

"Have you got enough on your plate?" Gray asked Ev as we walked around the self-serve area of the main restaurant.

"Nope. I'm sure I can fit some more in. Maybe a little slice of your attitude since you seem to have so much to spare," Ev replied, taking another plate and adding two bread rolls and some butter.

"Please, dude. You couldn't handle my attitude."

I snorted.

"You know you're allowed a second trip, right?" I said to both of them because, despite Gray's teasing, his plate was piled just as high.

"I know," they said simultaneously.

I shook my head and walked to the table. When we were all seated, the server came over to take our drink orders.

"I'll have the Peachy Sunset cocktail and a pitcher of water, please," Ev said.

I looked at the drinks menu and saw Ev had ordered the most expensive drink. Gray looked up from his menu and laughed.

"Same for me, please."

"Can I have a soda?" I asked.

"Of course, sir. Will that be all?" the server asked.

"Yes," I said.

"No," Ev and Gray responded.

"What? You want more drinks?" I asked.

"No, honey," Gray said. "You're ordering yourself a Piña Colada because that's your favorite." He looked at the server, who nodded and then left.

"Gray, have you seen how expensive these drinks are?"

"Yep. I have it on good account that drinks tonight are on my overprivileged ass."

I stared open-mouthed.

Ev laughed. "Serves him right for touching my stuff."

"If I'm not mistaken, you were the one doing all the touching," Gray replied.

What the fuck was going on? Were they…flirting?

"What's up, Felix? You look like you're having an aneurysm," Ev said.

I shook my head. "Nothing. Let's just eat before the drinks arrive. I don't think I can handle you both being nice to each other *and* drunk at the same time."

"What happens at the resort stays at the resort." Gray winked.

I started eating with the intention of going back for a second serving. Things were definitely getting weird around here, and I didn't like the little flutters of hope dancing in my belly.

My new plan was to eat as much as I could before throwing up so I could fall into a food coma as soon as we got back to the cottage.

"Good evening, gentleman. I'm Mallory Prescott, the resort manager. I take it you're having an enjoyable time with us?"

I looked up at the man that had approached our table. He had deep-blue eyes and dark hair peppered with some silver strands. Well-built but with a soft smile, he was undeniably gorgeous.

Wait… "Prescott?"

"That's right. If there are any problems, please, do let me know. We've just reopened after a major restoration, so I apologize in advance if you notice any unfinished touches. Hopefully, there won't be many of those."

"No…we haven't seen anything. Everything has been great, and everyone is so attentive. Thank you for asking," I said.

I looked at Ev, whose eyes were wide as he signaled to the hand Mallory had over the empty chair. He wore a wedding ring.

"I'll leave you to enjoy your dinner," Mallory said and moved on to speak to the diners at a different table.

"Oh my god, Felix. I thought you were joking earlier," Ev said.

"I was. No, that can't be him. How about the other guy Griffin was with?"

"Maybe he's having an affair."

"No. He wouldn't. He's a romance author, for Pete's sake. Besides, if you were having an affair, would you really take him to the place where your husband works?" I asked.

"Do you want to share with the table?" Gray

asked.

His plate was almost empty, and he looked ready to have some more.

"The author that wrote the book Ev is reading lives on the island. We saw him earlier with a guy. We assumed he was his husband, but now this guy says his last name is Prescott."

Gray stared at both Ev and me like we were crazy. "I need some food to unpick this. And if you see the server, please order more drinks."

We ignored him and leaned over the table as if we were sharing a secret.

"There are no photos on his social media, but I swear I've seen him mention his husband by name," Ev said.

I pulled my phone out and went on the Facebook app to Griffin Prescott's reader group.

The most recent posts were about how he'd taken some time off from writing to help his community and his…bingo. Someone commented on an old post, which bumped it up.

"Look, he's saying here Mal got a new job, so they're moving to the west coast. His husband's name is Mal…Mallory. That's him."

Gray came back with a plate stacked with desserts. "Okay, I'm ready for your crazy story."

I explained it to him while Ev left the table to

bring us both our desserts. He was just sitting down when Gray spoke again.

"What if he's with both men at the same time? It sounds like he wasn't exactly hiding the other dude, and you said they looked happy and relaxed as they walked on the beach."

I felt my skin heat up like a massive spotlight had been turned in my direction.

"Really?" Ev asked. "Is that a thing?"

Gray replied. "Sure is. I watched a documentary about it a while ago. It's probably more common than we think. I sure wouldn't mind being with two guys at once. Double the dick, double the fun. Triple the dick? Hell yeah."

A piece of cake lodged in my throat, and I coughed to push it out. Ev filled my glass with water and pushed it in my direction.

"You okay?" Gray asked.

"Yes. Yes…just…um…cake," I said between coughs.

"So I see," he said, raising a brow. Ev looked equally as puzzled.

I was perfectly okay. As okay as anyone would be when the object of their affection voiced exactly the one thing you dreamed about but thought you couldn't share with anyone.

Yup, I was perfectly fine. Peachy.

7

EVERETT

"I WANNA SEE THE BUNS. Yeah...the bun...bunnies!"

Gray looked at me and smiled. Felix was adorable when he had a few drinks, and this evening wasn't any different.

"You want to see the bunnies?" I asked.

"Yash. I read on the...the thing...what's the name?" Felix looked at Gray, and from his expression, he also had no idea what he was talking about.

"The folder!" Felix shouted before he almost tripped over his own feet. "In the kitchen."

We were walking back to the cottage. We'd gone to the bar after dinner, and this time, I insisted on paying for the drinks. Felix had already drunk more than usual, so both Gray and I made a silent agreement to change to non-alcoholic drinks and let Felix enjoy himself.

We kept him safe and made sure he didn't drink too much. He was just a lightweight, so the three Piña Coladas, even with a full dinner, were responsible for his current state.

"The folder," I repeated.

"Aren't you listening?" Felix asked, placing his hands on his hips as he stopped in the middle of the path.

Two guests from the resort smiled as they had to walk around us to avoid crashing into Felix.

"There are bunnies here. We can feed them," Felix said and then pointed a finger at us. "But not too much. There are pe…pe…pellets in the kitchen." He started walking again, and Gray and I followed him.

We exchanged a smile that made my belly flip a little. Gray was gorgeous at the best of times, but right now, there was something more to him I couldn't put my finger on. It was as if he looked different, which was ridiculous.

We followed in silence behind Felix, who'd picked up the pace as he talked endlessly about bunnies. I shook my head, envious of how easy it was for him to relax and let go.

As soon as we arrived at the cottage, Felix sat on

the chair outside and closed his eyes. "Hmm, cheese moon. I like cheese."

"Oh no, Sleeping Beauty, you're not falling asleep out here. We're taking you to bed," I said, pulling him to his feet while Gray got the door.

"Now you're talking." He leaned into me. His hair smelled of shampoo and beach, and it was so soft I wanted to run my fingers through it.

I caught Gray's eyes and saw him staring at us.

"Help me get him ready for bed," I said. He nodded.

We walked Felix to his bedroom, removed his clothes until he was only in his underwear, and then put him to bed, covering him with a bedsheet, which would be enough considering the nights were still fairly warm.

"Hmm, I like this…" Felix mumbled, half asleep.

"Like what?" Gray asked with a chuckle.

"You two, man…hmm…man…handle me. One…not enough…two…good…" That was all he said before he was asleep, snoring softly.

I picked up his clothes and placed them on a chair before we both walked out of the room.

"Maybe we should leave his door open a little in case he needs *us*," Gray said as we stood outside of Felix's bedroom door.

My belly did another flip at the way he said us. As

if we were both equally responsible for Felix. And that made me strangely happy.

I nodded. "I'll leave my door open too."

"Just don't jerk off," Gray said.

"You couldn't help yourself, could you?" I asked, shaking my head.

He chuckled and shrugged. "You're too easy."

I raised a brow. "Am I now?"

The air between us crackled. Gray's eyes stared at me in the same way he had the night of the Christmas party at Felix's. Did he want me? Did he *still* want me? But what about Felix?

Whether Gray remembered it or not, the words he'd said had become imprinted in my brain. *I think I'm in love with my best friend.* That had sealed the deal for me. I wouldn't stand between Gray and Felix, even if in the back of my mind there was a tiny voice that said my place was exactly between them, with them.

But that was crazy. Right?

"I better go to sleep," I said.

Gray opened his mouth as if he was going to say something but stopped himself.

"Yeah, you're right. Goodnight, Ev."

"Night, Gray."

As we went in opposite directions to our rooms, it dawned on me that had been the first time in over two years that we'd used each other's nicknames.

I tossed and turned in bed for the longest time before I could sleep. Felix would occasionally mumble something in his sleep that was loud enough for me to hear but not clear enough to understand.

When sleep finally came, I dreamed of home, family, Felix, and Gray.

And when I woke up, I knew I needed to push my feelings down before I got hurt.

Felix might end up hating me for it, but I was one step away from turning the corner on Heartbreak Lane. If I wanted to keep the most important thing in my life, Felix's friendship, I needed to be strong.

8

GRAYSON

History was repeating itself, and I had no clue how to change it.

Okay, so this time, I hadn't been kneed in the balls, but maybe it would have been better because then I'd have confirmation that Everett really did not like me.

The push-pull between us gave me whiplash, but I didn't want to upset Felix by fighting with Everett. No matter how frustrating he was.

I could have sworn that two nights ago, after we put Felix to bed, there was something between us. I'd been so close to kissing him, and it was only my fear of his reaction, coupled with not wanting to wake up Felix, which had stopped me.

I also could have sworn we were on the same page.

But the next morning, Everett had gone back to being distant with me, to the point he ignored my presence unless it was too obvious to Felix that that's what he was doing.

In the last two days, all Everett had done was lay on the fucking lounge chair reading his stupid books. Even Felix had come on a speedboat ride with me to visit the various rock formations and caves around the coastline of La Catarina island.

I wanted to shake up Everett. Badly. Unfortunately for him, I knew exactly how to do that.

"Good afternoon, sir. Your jet skis are ready," Ben, the guy running the water sports hut, said as he approached us. I gave him a tip and thanked him.

"Jet skis, Gray? Really?" Felix sighed, and I smiled.

"They're not for you, babe. Everett and I are going on an adventure."

"I can assure you, Everett is going nowhere with you," Ev said without looking up from his e-reader.

I laughed. "Luckily, you have your own jet ski, so you can ride as far away from me as your heart desires."

"I'd run out of gas too soon."

I straightened my back, pretending his words didn't have any effect on me.

"Come on, old man. Are you going to have some

fun on this vacation or decompose on that lounge chair? Are you thirty or seventy? My dad has better stamina."

He finally drew his gaze away from the e-reader to look at me. "There's nothing wrong with my stamina. I—"

"Prove it."

I stood up and walked to the edge of the water where Ben had left the jet skis.

A moment later, I heard footsteps on the sand. I knew he wouldn't back out of that challenge. I could see it in his eyes.

I put the safety jacket on and pushed my jet ski into the water before starting the motor. I stayed near the shore, waiting for Ev.

"Come on, what's taking so long? I'm growing white hairs here," I teased.

He flipped the bird and pushed his jet ski into the water. I thought I saw a moment of indecision as Ev stared at the jet ski and the water around us, but then he jumped on.

"Do you know how this works?"

He shook his head, looking at the controls. I maneuvered my jet ski so I was side to side with his. They bumped a little, which was fine, but suddenly Ev had a tight grip on my arm.

"Are you okay?" I asked.

"Yeah…um…I've just never done this before."

"Okay. We'll hook you up to the safety lanyard first. This means if you fall off the jet ski, it will stop too."

I ran through the commands to start up his jet ski and then demonstrated how to accelerate and use the water to reduce speed or break if needed.

He repeated everything back to me, so I knew he understood it. My intention had been to get Ev out of his lounge chair routine and pump some adrenaline into his body, but the way he'd clung to me before told me he was way out of his comfort zone. If all he did was ride the jet ski slowly, I'd be happy.

"Okay, I'll go first," I said and rode my jet ski away from the shore. Once I was a safe distance away from him, I stopped and looked back to watch.

Felix was on the shore looking at us with a worried expression, but there was nothing to worry about. Even kids rode these things unaccompanied, so I was sure nothing would happen.

Pride rose in my chest as Ev rode past me, slowly at first and then picking up a little speed. There was no other watercraft around us, creating waves or distracting us.

Ev looked so focused on his task, but as I rode closer to him, I could see him relax a little. He was starting to enjoy himself.

"Go, Ev!" Felix shouted from the beach.

"You're doing great, babe," I shouted loud enough for him to hear before I realized what I'd said.

Ev turned his jet ski and looked at me. Fuck, he'd heard me all right.

He was a few yards away from me, but I could still see the intensity in his gaze. That was it. As soon as we were back on land, I'd confront him about his behavior.

And then I'd kiss the shit out of him to shut him up. We were going to end this once and for all.

The noise of a motor broke out in the background, and out of nowhere, a speedboat drove past, creating some large waves just as Ev started his jet ski again.

My words got stuck in my throat as I watched Ev struggle with the waves and the movement of the jet ski. One moment he was on it, and the next, I couldn't see him.

I started up my jet ski and circled him carefully. He had a life jacket, so I knew he'd float, but falling on your first go was always a scary experience.

"Ev," I called.

He struggled in the water, his arms flapping, and he kept going under.

"Stay still. You'll float."

"Help!" he shouted. "Can't…" Some more coughing. "Swim…"

"Fuck."

9

FELIX

"No! Ev!"

Watching Ev disappear into the water behind his jet ski was terrifying. I knew Gray would get to him quick enough, but it wasn't until I saw Gray pull Ev out of the water and onto his own jet ski that I was able to take another breath.

Gray rode his jet ski until he was partially on the sand and then came off, helping Ev, who was coughing and struggling to breathe.

He kneeled and kept his head down.

"I'll call the medic," one of the guests nearby said.

A small crowd surrounded us to see what was going on, but one look from Gray and people dispersed.

"Ev, are you okay?" I said, running my hand over his hair to try to see his face. He was pale and had his eyes closed, but he was trying to steady his breathing. "Take deep breaths. That's it."

My eyes met Gray's over Ev. He was worried but also…angry? Why would he be angry? It was clear Ev had never ridden a jet ski, and accidents happened, right?

The lady came back with Ben and the medic.

I stepped back to give them some space while Gray spoke to Ben, who told him he'd take care of the jet skis. We didn't have to worry about anything.

My heart rate didn't decrease until the medic reassured us that Ev was okay. He hadn't taken in much water, and he had never lost consciousness, but we should let the medic know if anything changed.

"I'm so sorry," Ev said, looking at me. He tried to stand up, so I helped him, and then we walked toward the cottage.

"There's nothing for you to be sorry for, Ev. It was an accident. No one saw that stupid speedboat coming. I was standing on the shore, and even I missed it until I saw all the waves."

We walked inside the cottage, and Ev took a seat at the kitchen table. I grabbed a glass of water and put it in front of him.

A moment later, Gray walked in—the picture of rage—and stood in front of Ev.

"Why didn't you tell me, Ev? Do you have a death wish? Do you?"

Gray ran his hands over his hair and pulled, leaving his wavy locks all over the place.

"Told you what?" I asked.

"He can't fucking swim," Gray shouted. He turned around and put his hands on the kitchen sink, his knuckles going white from how hard he was gripping it.

I looked at Ev, who was staring at the floor. Once again, my words failed me.

This could have ended in tragedy. Ev could have died.

I walked back until I felt the kitchen counter and sagged against it, tears building in the back of my eyes.

Ev stood up and wrapped his arms around me. He felt cold to the touch, which reminded me exactly what could have happened.

"I'm sorry, Felix. I'm so sorry," he whispered in my ear.

He let go and turned to face Gray, who was staring out of the window with his jaw clenched tight. I knew he felt responsible because, even if he didn't know that Ev couldn't swim, he was the one who'd challenged him.

Ev touched Gray's arm, and he turned around but pulled away from Ev's touch.

"I— " Ev started but was interrupted by Gray.

"Why didn't you say something? Why did you take my challenge?" The anger from before had subsided a little, and all I could see in Gray's eyes was worry.

"Because I'm an asshole. I should have backed out. God knows I haven't so much as wet my feet in the last few days, but…" He took in a long breath and looked at me briefly before turning back to Gray. "I didn't want you to see me as less than…weak, boring. I wanted…"

"What did you want, Ev?"

They stared at each other for the longest time until Ev put his hand behind Gray's neck and pulled him closer, slamming their lips together.

I gasped and watched as Gray stilled but gave in. And when I say gave in, I mean, gave up.

What I'd known all along became clear as glass at that moment. Gray and Ev, despite the fighting and the bickering, liked each other. Probably more than either cared to admit.

I took a step back to give them space, but Ev's hand curled around my wrist, and then he stopped kissing Gray.

Their lips were moist and red. Both looked

equally confused, as if they were surprised that they liked kissing each other.

Ev looked at me. "If I'm finally kissing someone I don't like, then I sure am kissing someone I do." And then, in the same way that he'd taken Gray's mouth, Ev claimed mine.

The only difference was that it felt gentler, more reverent. As if this was his only chance ever to taste me and he wanted it to count. I felt exactly the same way.

A different mouth latched on to my neck and sucked gently. Gray...

I wanted to get my head around what was happening. How did we get here? But I couldn't stop kissing Ev. He tasted too good. His lips were far too soft.

He was the one that put some distance between our lips. I took a moment before I opened my eyes, just in case this wasn't real. If it was a fantasy, I didn't want it to end.

Ev's eyes were on Gray. I looked at Gray, and he was staring at me.

There was no question about what my next move was. I turned around to face Gray and put my arms around his shoulders. That gave me the little extra height I needed to reach his mouth.

Gray's kiss was different from Ev's but no less

amazing. He took his time sucking each of my lips before demanding entry with his warm tongue.

I moaned when I felt Ev's lips on the back of my neck. They held on to each other, keeping me tight between them.

I was being ravished by the two men I'd wanted for longer than I cared to imagine.

"Fuck, Felix," Gray whispered into my mouth, and then he raised his head to look at Ev again. "Everett, you fucking fuck."

I chuckled and watched as they kissed again, this time slower.

Yep, I had to be dreaming.

10

EVERETT

I COULD PUT the first kiss down to the adrenaline of thinking I was going to drown, then being rescued by Gray and seeing how angry he was because he hadn't known I couldn't swim.

All the emotions swirling inside me had finally found their way out through the cracks, and I hadn't thought anything of going up to Gray and kissing the hell out of him.

And as soon as Felix pulled away, I knew I couldn't let him get away. I had one chance to show him what I wanted.

But that second kiss with Gray? That sealed my fate.

That one wasn't adrenaline-fueled. No, that was all powered by my heart and pent-up chemistry that had been there from the day Felix had introduced us.

We were the same height, so his lips had been there, only a few inches away, still wet from his kiss with Felix and begging for more.

Felix was so close to us that I felt the breath he let out on my cheek.

I let go of Gray with some reluctance and loved it when he tried to chase my lips before I turned to Felix. "Did you like watching us?"

His cheeks went adorably pink, which only made me want to kiss him more. If there was ever a word that would describe Felix, that word was adorable. His smaller frame, combined with his don't-mess-with-the-teacher attitude, was incredibly sexy, but his big heart was everything.

He nodded and then looked at Gray.

"What's happening?" Felix asked and then closed his eyes and shook his head. "I mean, I know what just happened, but I don't understand."

Gray released the hold he had on me, and I figured he did the same with Felix because his face dropped.

"Hey," Gray said, cradling Felix's cheek with his hand. "We just need to talk before this escalates, okay?"

"Escalates?"

Gray looked at me, winked, and then pulled Felix closer, placing his hand on Felix's lower back so they were facing each other again. Even from where I stood, I could tell there wasn't a breath of air between them.

"You feel that, Felix?" Gray asked. "That's for you and the asshole behind you. I'm not sure I understand what's going on. So yeah, we need to talk before I drag you both to the king-size bed in my room, and we do something we might regret."

"You have a king-size bed?" I asked.

Felix stared at me. "That's what you took from that?"

"Hell yeah," I said. "Grayson Davenport has a hard-on for me, so he can call me whatever he wants, but a fucking king-size bed? I've been sleeping with my feet over the edge of the bed because it's so small."

"You picked your room, remember?"

Gray groaned his frustration and pulled us toward the lounge area. He stood in front of the couch, staring at it for a moment.

"You don't need to ask for permission, you know?" I teased.

He elbowed me and then pushed so I fell at one end of the couch. I thought he'd sit at the other end and have Felix between us, but he surprised me by sitting next to me and pulling Felix onto his lap.

Felix squealed when I grabbed his legs and draped them over mine.

"I should probably go first since I initiated this," I said.

"No," Felix said, holding both my and Gray's hands with his. "I did."

He kept his gaze on our joined hands, and I squeezed to get his attention. When he looked up, all I saw was uncertainty, and I didn't like that at all.

"I asked you both to come on this vacation and didn't tell you the other was coming, on purpose," he said.

"It's understandable. I'm sure neither of us would have come if we'd known," Gray said.

"Why?" Felix asked.

Gray looked at me. "Isn't it obvious? Ev doesn't... didn't like me." And then he turned to me. "Why? Why did you suddenly change? We used to be friends."

I let out a sigh. So we were having this conversation here and in front of Felix.

Heck, I'd already kissed them both, so nothing would ever be the same anyway.

"Remember the Christmas party?" I asked.

"Like it was yesterday. You have no idea how many times I played that night in my head to figure out what I did wrong to make you hate me."

"Wait," Felix interrupted. "What Christmas party? The one at my place two years ago?"

I nodded. "Gray, you drank, and we flirted. There was this insane chemistry between us, but then you said you loved Felix."

"What?"

"What?"

Felix and Gray spoke simultaneously, looking at me and then at each other.

"I could tell you still wanted me, but fuck, you said the L-word. How could I get between you and my best friend? So I put some distance between us. You didn't take the rejection too well, and the rest is history."

Gray opened his mouth to speak, but Felix interrupted. "Wait. Gray, is that true?"

"Yes. I'm sorry, I don't remember some of that, but it's true, Felix. I do love you." Then Gray turned to me. "But I've also felt this unexplained attraction to you."

I shook my head, and Gray took my hand in his.

"Ev, I didn't think I loved you then because we hadn't known each other as long. But it didn't mean I wouldn't, or that...I don't."

I couldn't make sense of what he was saying. Was Gray confessing to having feelings for me beyond attraction? And why wasn't I jealous that he'd confirmed he loved Felix? Why did that also make me happy?

I removed Felix's legs from my lap and stood up, needing a little distance to make sense of everything.

"Please don't go," Felix said. "I'm in love with both of you."

He stood up from Gray's lap and faced us both. "I love you so much it hurts. And I can't choose. I've been trying to choose one of you for years and I can't. When I introduced you, I hoped you'd be friends, and maybe one day I could tell you the truth. It was great in the beginning. Even if you couldn't see it, I could. You both talked about each other all the time. You asked about each other. I hoped….I was ready to tell you that night. But then you both disappeared, and nothing was the same ever again."

He ran his hand through his short hair. "If you don't totally hate each other, do you think…maybe…"

11

GRAYSON

I DIDN'T HATE EVERETT. Far from it. His kiss had awakened a part of me I'd been trying to deny for a long time.

Despite our weird feud, I'd never been able to let go. He didn't know I was the one who'd ordered food from his favorite restaurant when he got sick one time when Felix was away on a school trip.

He didn't know the other, more important, stuff I did for him. I knew my time was running out, but I couldn't tell him just yet.

I knew he'd do the same for me if the roles were reversed. I didn't need to ask. I just knew it.

And since when the fuck did I become a sappy, emotional, romantic, lovesick puppy?

I sighed.

We were at an impasse, and I knew I'd need to be

the one to take the first step. Felix needed me to do it, and Ev needed me to do it.

I stood up and stretched a hand out to Felix. He took it and didn't bat an eye when I pulled him close enough that I could just tilt his head up if I wanted a kiss.

Which I did, so I kissed him gently.

"I love you, Felix. Do you feel the same way?"

He nodded. "Would it bother you if I said I love Ev too?"

I shook my head and saw the unshed tears in his eyes. I wondered how long he'd been alone with all these feelings.

"Ev," I said, stretching my other hand. "Come here, baby."

He didn't come as quickly as Felix. I assumed he was still trying to protect himself, but I would prove to him that he didn't need to be afraid.

When he did come, I treated him the same as Felix but let the kiss linger a little longer.

Felix kissed Ev when I released him, and then we just stood there, hugging, like we'd just found each other again after years of separation.

How had we not realized that something was broken?

Neither seemed to be keen to stop the contact, but having the two men pressed against me was definitely having a not entirely undesirable effect. The question was, were they ready to take the next step?

"Guys, in case no one noticed, we're all half-naked. In case no one noticed, we all are into each other. And in case no one noticed, things are stirring in my shorts," I said.

"We noticed," they both said.

"How about we have a shower, get dressed, and go out for an early dinner?" I suggested.

Felix gave me the most adorable smile.

I planted a kiss on his lips and said, "Shower separately, or we'll never leave." I looked at Ev, whose gaze was lust personified. "You know if we start this, we won't stop for a while. Help me out here, Ev."

"Not in my best interests," he said.

I groaned and let go of them both, running to my room and going straight for the shower. The water was blissfully cold because my dick needed to calm the fuck down.

A moment later, the shower door opened behind me, and they both came inside. Naked.

"You also have the biggest shower," Ev complained.

"I remind you, you picked your room," Felix said.

I rested my head on the tiles and reached the water tap. It was warming up too quickly. Or maybe it was the effect of having two sexy men naked with me.

A pair of hands ran down my back, caressing and massaging. I didn't know if it was both or only one of them.

I looked behind me and got my answer. They were kissing while touching me, and that made my dick even harder than it had been.

"You're fucking terrible," I said, turning around.

"No, baby," Ev said. "We're just fucking."

He slammed his mouth onto mine in a bruising kiss that took my breath away.

Since Ev was consuming me like I was the best meal he'd ever had, I knew the mouth that engulfed my dick in red-hot heat was Felix's.

"Hmm...ahh." I had to stop the kiss to take in some air because it all felt so good. I looked down and saw the water sluicing over Felix's back and down the crease of his perfect ass.

There was so much for us to figure out about being together—or whatever we were doing—but there was no way eating Felix's ass wasn't in my future.

"We can share, right?" Ev asked as if he guessed the direction my thoughts were headed.

I looked at him and was going to say hell yeah, but Felix decided that was the best time to take my dick in all the way down until I felt the head hit the back of his throat.

"Jesus, fuck, don't you have a gag reflex?"

He shook his head as he drew back out and then looked at me like butter wouldn't melt.

Ev had his hand wrapped around his dick, so I swatted it away and replaced it with mine. His cock was a work of art. Long, thick, with a thatch of dark hair and a purple head that I couldn't wait to taste.

"Gray," Ev called when instead of just jerking him off, I took my time, twisting my wrist and varying the amount of pressure I applied to his shaft.

We had to make this quick because the shower was not the place for us to explore each other properly. Not that I'd have a problem making it quick. I was as close to bursting as I'd ever been, and Ev's eyes were rolled back in pleasure.

"Fuck, Gray, your hand feels so good." He hissed when I dragged my nail over the slit. "Hmm, like that, fuck, I'm so close."

"Me too, baby."

Felix let go of my cock and stood up, replacing his mouth with his hand.

"Me three."

Ev's hand went for Felix's dick before we took turns kissing each other. Or as much as we could kiss when we were all panting as if we were running a marathon and moaning louder than porn stars.

We came in a slur of curses loud enough to make a sailor blush.

As we each came down to earth from the shattering orgasms, we made out and washed each other. It was hands down the best experience of my life.

I didn't know what I needed to do to keep this, to keep them, but I'd do it. I'd even confront my father if necessary.

And if he insisted I left the company, I'd do it in a heartbeat.

Yup, that was how deep I already was.

12

FELIX

They were trying to kill me. It was the only explanation.

I groaned as I narrowly avoided spraining my foot on a loose rock.

"May I remind you that my lifestyle includes short walks, and when I say short, I mean the five steps I take from my desk to the blackboard at school and the two minutes to the teacher's lounge and the cafeteria. It also includes reruns of ALF and eating marshmallow fluff from the jar. My lifestyle does not include this kind of torture."

"Uh-huh," Gray and Ev said behind me.

I turned around just in time to catch them staring at my ass before they looked up at my face. They hadn't even been listening to me.

They both shrugged like they weren't sorry they

made me come on a hike to the stupid mountain just so we could see the bunnies.

Okay, fine, so it wasn't a mountain, it was a small grassy hill, and the view was amazing, even if we hadn't yet seen any bunnies.

"Baby, I'd walk five thousand miles behind your ass any day," Gray said.

"Word," Ev agreed.

I couldn't deny their words gave me a boost in confidence. I was a regular kind of guy. No abs, no muscles, no particular sense of fashion. I was short compared to Gray and Ev, so having them look at me as though they really liked what they saw was empowering.

"What if I want to walk behind your fine asses?" I asked. "At least I'd be in the shade."

Ev took a step forward and pulled me into his chest. "Maybe we should take it in turns."

I placed my hands on his chest and sighed in contentment. Gray came to his side and placed an arm around Ev's waist while reaching out to give me a kiss. "I can get on board with that."

It was incredible how two years of tension had disappeared like a droplet of water in the sun. Ev and Gray were no longer pretending to dislike each other. In fact, last night, as we were having the dinner we'd ended up ordering in, I caught them exchanging multiple heated looks.

I'd also been on the receiving end of those looks from both of them.

We'd agreed that it was a good idea to take things slow, despite our out-of-this-world shower orgasms. After all, we were all transitioning from being friends—or quasi-enemies—to lovers, and none of us wanted to damage our existing relationships.

Yes, Gray and I had voiced our feelings for each other and Ev, but Ev hadn't done the same.

I knew it would take him longer. He'd always had to fight hard for what he wanted, so he protected his belongings with fierce strength. His heart had the hardest shell of protection around it.

The proof of that was the way in which he'd stepped back under his perceived belief that he'd be in the way of something between Gray and me.

So, after dinner, we'd watched a movie and made out before going to our separate rooms.

"You know," I said. "I won't complain if your hands slide down my back and…you know…"

Gray groaned. "Baby, don't tease. Do you have any idea how hard it is to not jump both of you right now? I've had a hard-on since yesterday."

Ev agreed. "It's not comfortable. Or healthy. Especially when you have to sleep in a child's bed."

I rolled my eyes. "Fine, you can sleep in my bed, and I'll sleep in yours."

Ev stared at me, and it was so hard to keep a straight face.

"But…" He looked at Gray, who shrugged, and then back at me. "Fine."

I kissed the dejected look on his face. He wouldn't be sleeping in my bed tonight, and I wouldn't be sleeping in his because I fully planned to claim Gray's big bed for the three of us.

We were adults entering a relationship, right? No harm in having some fun while we worked out the kinks of how it would work. Besides, we still hadn't discussed what would happen when we got back to New York.

That was a conversation I was dreading because I was scared. What if life got in the way? What if people didn't understand the way we were together? Or accepted it?

"Look, isn't that the guy from the resort? What was his name? Matthew?" Gray asked.

"Mallory," I said. I turned around, and sure enough, Mallory was only a few feet away, walking with one arm around Griffin Prescott and the other arm around the guy we'd seen with Griffin.

"Gray, you were right," Ev said.

"Baby, I'm rarely wrong, but what am I right about this time?"

I laughed at the pointed look Ev sent Gray's way. If this way of communication was their foreplay, I couldn't wait to be there when it all came out in the bedroom.

"You said it was possible that Mallory, Griffin, and the other guy were all together."

"Shh, they're coming this way," I said.

We put a little distance from each other, but then I felt Ev and Gray pull me closer and rolled my eyes. I also felt like I'd just been claimed, and I was very much okay with that.

"Good morning, gentlemen. I see you're exploring the island," Mallory said. "Hope you're having fun."

There was an amused tone to his voice.

"We sure are, Mr. Prescott," I said when neither Gray nor Ev said anything. I looked up at them, and they were staring at Griffin and the other guy. I didn't blame them at all. Both men were stunning.

"Please call me Mal. These are my husbands, Griff and Jake."

My mouth dropped open. Did he just…?

"I recognize you," Griff said. "You're in my reader group. You're the teacher. Felix, right?"

I nodded because I was scared my brain messed

up the words I was supposed to say when meeting my favorite author.

"Babe, Felix is a teacher in New York. We ran an event last year to donate books with LGBTQ+ representation to schools around the country," Griff said.

"I remember you talking about it," Mal said. "Thank you for your support, Felix."

"There was a big team…I…I mean…I only coordinated a small part." I was pretty sure my face was beet red, and I couldn't just blame the sun. I'd never been very good at having a spotlight on me. That was why I became a teacher. I wanted to make a difference through my students.

"Don't undersell yourself," Jake said. "I wasn't with Mal and Griff at the time, but I can tell you if Griff remembers you, it is for a good reason."

I leaned against Ev, who tightened his hold on me.

"Can I ask you a question?" Gray asked. "You said they're your husbands. I don't want to seem rude, but…" He looked at Ev and me. "How does it work?"

13

EVERETT

I wanted a hole to appear in front of us and swallow us in one go. I couldn't believe Gray had asked that question. And to the man in a relationship with someone that Felix and I idolized so much.

"It's not rude at all," Mal said. "We all start somewhere, and I wish poly relationships had more representation so when people find themselves falling for more than one person, it doesn't feel like such a mountain to climb all on your own."

Griff nodded. "Technically, Mal and I are married. We were already before we met Jake. But as you know, marriage between more than two people is illegal. In fact, while you can't get fired for being gay, you can legally be fired for being in a relationship with two people."

Griff looked at Jake, who placed a soft kiss on his temple.

"We're lucky to be accepted here on the island. My uncle actually owns the resort, and both Mal and I work for the business. I know many people aren't as lucky. But to answer your question, the way it works is that we don't focus on what we are to each other legally." He looked at Mal, and his smile contained so much love that I had to look away.

I needed to think about how I really felt about both my men and the fact I thought about them as mine alone was telling.

"We love each other, and we have a relationship built on communication and trust. Well, that and we can't stay away from each other's pants," Jake said, laughing. He was joined by Griff, but Mal looked shocked for a second before he shook his head.

"What he means is that we felt that calling Jake our boyfriend would make a distinction between what we are to each other and what he is, when in fact we're all equal. Whether we're legally married or not, it doesn't matter to us. We're a unit," Mal said.

"Thank you," Gray said.

The three men left us with an invite to join them for dinner at the resort on our last night, which we accepted, and then there was just us.

Three guys who, until yesterday, had harbored

secret feelings for each other. Three guys who couldn't be more different but somehow fit together perfectly.

"No sudden moves," Felix whispered. "Look over there by the abandoned house."

Three bunnies chomped on the grass by the house. We'd seen the house earlier, and because it looked abandoned, Felix had said he wanted to get a closer look.

"Do you think they live in the house?" Gray asked.

"Who knows. That folder in the cottage mentioned the island is home to thousands of bunnies. Maybe they live here, maybe they just like hanging out," I said.

"They're so adorable," Felix said. He took his phone out and took a few photos of the bunnies. I then took the phone from him and flipped the camera to get a few snaps of the three of us.

"Our first official photos," Gray joked, but his face took on a different, more contemplative expression as he stared at the bunnies again.

Felix was still between us but was now leaning against Gray, who wrapped his arms around his shoulders. He looked happier than I'd seen him in a long time, maybe ever.

Mal's words about their relationship being based

on communication and trust were still running through my head on a loop.

I couldn't take my eyes off the two men in front of me. The men I was certain I wanted to build a life with, but before that happened and the last wall came down, I needed to come clean.

"Can we go back to the cottage?" I asked.

They both looked at me in surprise.

"Sure. Are you okay?" Felix asked, running his hands up and down my arms.

"Yeah…I just need to tell you something."

The walk back down to the resort didn't take as long, for which I was thankful because the longer I didn't get stuff off my chest, the more likely I was to back down and pretend it wasn't happening.

It was close to lunchtime, so Felix ordered room service to the cottage as soon as we got in.

Gray settled on the couch first. He sat forward with his elbows resting over his knees and his head held down. Felix plopped down next to him with a grim expression.

"I love you," I blurted out.

Both their heads snapped up.

Fuck, that's not how I wanted to start this conversation.

Gray pulled me onto his lap with such fierce strength, I had no option but to straddle him.

"What's going on, baby. You're scaring me. Us."

"But we love you," Felix said. "You know that, right?"

I nodded. "Um…before this vacation, I made the decision to sell my uncle's store and move upstate."

"What? Why?" Gray asked.

"Gray, this…is really difficult for me to say, especially to you, because it hurts like hell, but like Mal said, we need to communicate."

"Baby, nothing you say will change how I feel about you."

"Your father's company, your company, has been putting pressure on me to sell the store for months. They own the rest of the building. Apparently, they have planning permission to make the upper floors luxury apartments, and I guess the store would be perfect for the lobby area."

"No," Felix said, his voice rising. "You can't move. Not now, and not to fucking upstate."

I tried to get off Gray's lap, but he held my hips in place with strength I didn't know he had.

"I don't have a choice. Maybe I can come visit you on the weekends or something," I said.

"I'm not having a part-time relationship with you, Everett," Felix said. "You've been there for me for the longest time, and we were just friends. Now that we're more, or, well, becoming more, you're leaving us?

What is the point of telling us that you love us? So it can hurt more?"

Every single one of Felix's words was a dagger to my heart. He was right, but it wasn't like I wanted to leave. I was being forced out.

"Shh, calm down, baby," Gray said, pulling Felix closer, which meant he was also closer to me.

I raised my hand to cup his face, but he leaned away from me.

"Ev, what exactly do you mean when you say my father's company has been putting pressure on you?"

"I've been getting letters to vacate the store. I read and reread my lease, and I know they can't do it just like that. In the start, I ignored them, but they've become more persistent. They said all the other tenants of the apartments above are waiting on me to receive their settlement to leave. I know a woman upstairs who has a sick kid. She could get him the right treatment if she had the money. I have to accept it."

"No, you don't," Gray said.

"You don't understand. I have no choice. You should know, your father owns the fucking company."

Gray looked at me with dark steely eyes. "My father owns Davenport Corporation, but Grayson Davenport owns your building."

14

GRAYSON

Ev MADE a move to get off my lap, but this time I let him because I needed to drop a less than expertly crafted message to my lawyer.

Yeah, he was not going to be pleased. I guess no one was when they were threatened with losing their job.

"Give me one moment. Ev, please, if you love me and Felix like you said you do, please don't run."

He looked at me as if I'd assessed his intentions correctly.

"Baby, sit on him if you need to," I said to Felix before I kissed him and got up off the couch.

I ran to my room and took my phone from my carry-on luggage. I hadn't turned it on since I'd left New York. I stared at it for a moment as everything became clear.

I didn't just need this vacation to escape from the corporate world or from my family and the responsibilities of being a Davenport. I needed this vacation to find myself.

My parents, for all the time they dedicated to the company, had never foregone their time together. Why had I grown up behaving like I had to give every single second of my life to it?

Maybe I needed to spend some time thinking about that, but it was changing. That I knew for sure because I wanted to leave the office each night and step into the arms of the men I loved, my new family.

I turned the phone on and ignored the missed calls and messages from my assistant. If anything was really urgent, she would have called the resort to reach me.

I typed the message to my lawyer as quickly as I could and turned the phone back off.

When I returned to the living room, neither Ev nor Felix was there, but a quick search found Ev's bedroom door open.

I went inside and was surprised to see Ev had direct access to a small garden.

"You complain about the size of your bed when you have this garden? Dude, I pity you no more," I said.

"Not the time, Gray," Ev said.

I kneeled in front of him on the soft grass and put my hands on his knees so he had no choice but to look at me.

Felix sat on the chair opposite, looking so sad that I just wanted to pick him up and hold him, but we needed to deal with the current non-crisis first.

"Okay, it's time *I* come clean," I said.

"I thought you just did. You want me out of my business and my home. Great way to love someone, Gray."

"I have a lot of contacts in the city. A while ago, I heard some rumors about the owner of a building in Brooklyn wanting to sell. I don't know what made me look into it, but I did. I realized it was your building, so I bought it. I did all the paperwork through the company and used the company lawyer because he's also my lawyer for my personal affairs. The wires may have been crossed, but there's no question that the building belongs to me. Not to my dad or the corporation."

Ev looked at me. I couldn't tell what he was feeling, but I could tell he was trying to take everything in.

"And how about the letters?" Felix asked.

"I think that's where the wires got crossed. I don't know what happened, but I'll find out. One thing I can guarantee. You're not being kicked out of your business or your home. In fact, I was thinking of moving in."

"You…were?" Ev said, his eyes finally showing some emotion.

"Did you know the top floor in your building is empty and has an amazing roof garden? I haven't seen it personally, but I've seen the plans, and I've seen photos. I want to refurbish the top floor into one single apartment and move in. You already live there, and Felix is just around the corner." I rested my forehead on his lap. "I'm so tired of being on my own. Every day is the same. I work, I head off to a bar where I know I'll bump into someone I need to close a deal with or socialize, and then I go home to a fancy apartment that is as warm and welcoming as the polar caps."

Tears built in the back of my eyes. How had I never realized how lonely I was?

A hand rested on my head and another ran down my back. I looked up, and Ev cupped my cheek. Felix was right there next to me.

"I believe you, and I trust you, Gray," Ev said. "Many times I wanted to ask you about the letters, but I was afraid to find out you were behind it. I guess, even though things weren't good between us, I wanted to hold on to the Gray I knew, not a heartless corporate suit."

"Thank you, and I'm so sorry all this happened and that you thought you were going to lose everything."

"Shh, it's okay, we're good, aren't we?"

I raised my head to look at him. His eyes were warm and full of love. His lips were red, likely because he'd been biting on them while I spoke. And I wanted nothing more than to kiss them, make them red and plump from being loved, not worried.

The doorbell rang, so Felix got up to get it. It was probably our lunch delivery.

"Are you hungry?" Ev asked.

"Not particularly."

"What do you say we put lunch in the fridge and go test that big bed of yours?"

I stood up so fast I nearly got dizzy, but I recovered quickly and grabbed Ev by the hand, pulling him indoors.

15

FELIX

I'D BARELY CLOSED the cottage door when the bag with our lunch was unceremoniously taken from my hand, and I was lifted onto someone's shoulders.

Not someone…Gray. I'd know his ass from a lineup any time. After all, I'd been admiring it for years.

"What's going on?" I squeaked when a hand made contact with my butt.

"Do we need to spell it out, baby?" Gray said, walking out of the kitchen. "I keep being told how unfair it is that I have the biggest bed here. I think it's time to share it."

"Damn right," Ev said.

Gray dropped me on the bed and covered my body with his.

"Do you have any idea how long I've wanted to

have you like this?" he said, running his nose along the side of my neck and inhaling.

I knew because I'd wanted it as long, if not longer.

He lifted his hips, and I felt rather than saw his clothes being removed.

"Lift up a little," he said. Since his hands were busy cradling my face as he peppered me with kisses, there were no guesses as to who had been tasked with undressing us all.

Gray only stopped kissing me when he had to get on his knees so Ev could help him out of his shirt. I took mine off and then admired the two guys in front of me.

Ev's strong, wide chest tapered down into a small waist and abs that went on for days. My mouth watered at the sight of his hard cock pointing upward. How he had time to work out that body, I had no idea because he seemed to be in his store all the time, but I didn't care. I just wanted to lick him everywhere. Especially his cock.

I'd never been more thankful for my lack of gag reflex than now because I had full intentions of working my two men up with my mouth.

And then there was Gray, with his swimmer's body. He was strong, tight, and even if he wasn't as built as Ev, he didn't lack in the abs department.

I would have felt inadequate in their presence if it wasn't for the way they were looking at me.

"I don't even know where to start," Ev said.

I reached down to my cock and squeezed at the root before dragging my hand up and down my shaft.

"Fuck…" Gray said, his voice husky and full of need. "You take the bottom. I take the top. Meet in the middle."

"Got it," Ev said.

"Way to make a guy feel like a piece of—fuck!" I raised my hips involuntarily because as Gray engulfed my dick in the heat of his mouth, Ev went for the kill by opening my legs and licking a path from my ass up to my balls.

They were consuming me and making me feel everything I never thought I'd experience in my life. And this was just the beginning.

I raised my head and saw Ev meet Gray's lips around my cock, which couldn't be harder. They stared into each other's eyes as they slowly made their way up to the head. The way they were both sucking made my head spin, but watching as they kissed and tasted each other afterward got me close to busting.

"You look so sexy together," I rasped. "It's like my own personal porn show."

Even as they kissed, I saw Ev raise a brow and then whisper something in Gray's ear.

Gray groaned, and then they changed their position so they were head to toe right in front of me. I scooted over a little to watch the show as they went down on each other.

"Jesus, fuck. I think I can come just watching you two," I said. I didn't notice my hands made their way down to stroke my cock until Ev, who was on top of Gray and sucking his cock like a lollipop, pushed my hand away and replaced it with his.

After what felt like a hundred years, they came up for air and stretched out on either side of me.

"Hmm, Felix sandwich," Ev said, sucking a patch of skin on my neck. It was definitely going to leave a mark. The bastard.

"Erm…guys…I…" Their rock-hard dicks were pressing against my sides. I wanted them inside me so badly, but I didn't know how to ask for it.

"Nothing happens that we all don't consent to, Felix," Ev said.

"I know, it's just…I want…" I covered my face with my hands. Heat rising up my neck. Why was I suddenly embarrassed?

"What do you want, Felix? Tell us," Gray asked.

I looked at them and saw no judgment, just love and a whole lotta lust.

Ev lowered his mouth to my nipple and sucked it

into a peak. "Do you want me to fuck you while Gray fucks me?"

I let out a sound I couldn't even describe.

Gray followed in Ev's trail and did the same to the other nipple. "Do you want to fuck me while I fuck Ev?"

"Ugh…fuck…"

"That's not an answer, baby," Gray said.

"I want you both to fuck me," I blurted out and then put my hands over my face.

I felt them still over me, and even though I couldn't see them, I knew they had a silent exchange.

"Felix, are you sure?" Ev asked. He took my hands away from my face, and I looked into his dark eyes.

"Yes."

"Have you ever done it before?" Gray asked.

I bit my lip. "Technically, yes…and no?"

16

EVERETT

I couldn't deny my dick jumped for joy when Felix blurted out that he wanted both me and Gray inside him. It's not something I'd ever thought about, but since I'd come more times than I could remember to fantasies of both Felix and Gray, I wasn't surprised that the thought of the three of us together in that way got me all worked up.

"Define technically," I said.

Felix had a deep blush on his skin, and I could tell that while this was something he really wanted, he was unsure about asking.

"I've...um...used two dildos in my ass at the same time before. I...I pretended it was both of you taking me. I never thought we'd ever...I mean, we don't have to. Anything we do is going to be amazing.

I know it. I just, I don't know why, but I need our first time together to really be our first time *together*."

His voice went quieter toward the end of his ramble and his eyes were full of uncertainty.

The look Gray sent my way told me we were both on the same page. He turned over so he was on his back and took Felix with him. I placed a few pillows behind his back to raise him a little.

"Fuck, you look so good like that," I said. "One day, I want to see you ride Gray, Felix. And I'm going to watch until I'm so hard I could come from a breath of air, but I'll wait until you're both ready before I spill all over you."

I took his mouth into a bruising kiss and didn't let go until Felix moved his hips so his cock rubbed against Gray's.

"Condoms. Washbag," Gray managed to say before I stopped kissing Felix to kiss him.

"I'll get them."

I'd always looked after myself and others. Even in my business, I'd hired people that needed more than just a job. So it was no surprise that I took on the role of caring for both of my men.

"Lift up, baby," I said to Felix so I could get to Gray's cock. He was hard and leaking, and I couldn't resist sucking his crown.

"Fuck, Ev. Do you want me to come right now?"

I chuckled and suited him up before rolling a condom down my cock.

I took my place behind Felix and pushed him forward to lean on top of Gray, which gave me the perfect view of his tight hole.

Once again, I couldn't resist having a taste. Felix moaned.

"Ev!" they both shouted.

"Aren't you so impatient today?"

"I swear to god, Ev. If you don't—" Felix's words were stuck when I applied a good amount of lube on his hole and pushed a finger in.

We'd need to go slow because I didn't want to hurt Felix, and I knew Gray didn't want that either. We were both well endowed, and hell, two dicks in a small hole is still two dicks in a small hole.

When Felix started riding my finger, I added another one, and it didn't take long for him to push back, needing more.

"Are you ready for Gray?" I asked.

"Yes, please, yes."

I lined up Gray's cock with Felix's hole and nearly came at the sight of it disappearing inch by inch.

"Jesus Christ. This is torture," I groaned.

"Try being inside him. It feels so good, baby," Gray said.

Felix had his face in the crook of Gray's neck, and the only sounds coming from him were moans.

It looked impossible to add my cock to an already tight space. How would it ever fit?

"Baby, are you sure about this?" I asked.

"Just go slow, but please, do it. I need it, Ev. I need you," Felix said, looking back at me.

I added more lube and lined up my cock with Gray's. He was all the way in, and they were both very still. Waiting for me.

Felix put his arm behind his back and reached for me. I took his hand and he squeezed mine to reassure me he was ready. I pushed through the resisting muscles. It took a moment, but when I was finally inside, even if it was just my head, I thought I was going to explode from pleasure.

Strangely my first thought was how amazing it would be if we didn't need condoms. If both Gray and I could leave a little bit of us behind inside Felix.

I pushed the thought aside because it was a sure way to make me come sooner than I wanted. I added a little more of my length, and then Gray moved too.

"Fuck, fuck, fuck." I shouted.

"Did you come?" he asked.

"No, you fucker. But I will if you don't stop that."

Felix chuckled, and then Gray reached behind Felix. I took his hand and kissed it.

Our eyes met, and as I found myself all the way inside Felix, I knew there was no way back for us. Ever.

"I love you," I whispered.

"Love you too, baby."

Felix let out a whimper.

"Are you ready for more, baby?" I asked.

He nodded.

I put my arm around his chest and pulled him to me. His cock was so hard and the purple head was leaking.

He rested his head on my shoulder, his green eyes rolled back in pleasure even though we were barely moving inside him.

I sucked the skin on his neck to match the mark I'd left him on the other side earlier and then saw Gray grip Felix's cock.

He nodded, and I withdrew my cock almost all the way before pushing it in again.

I gritted my teeth at how amazing it felt. It was tight, hot, and unlike anything I'd ever experienced before.

"Oh my god, oh my god," Felix shouted as both Gray and I moved in synchronicity.

It was too good, too perfect, and I knew it would end all too soon.

"Are you ready to let go, Felix?" Gray asked.

"Yes," he said but shook his head. I knew the feeling because I was on the edge, but I wanted this to last forever.

"We'll be here to catch you, baby," Gray said,

I whispered in Felix's ear, "I love you so much, baby. We'll do this again, I promise. We have a lifetime of this perfection ahead of us."

I don't know if it was our words or the fact that every time I pushed inside Felix it made Gray's cock brush up against his prostate, but Felix stilled and then let out the most beautiful guttural sound before spilling all over Gray's stomach.

That sight, alongside the way Felix's hole was spasming around us, started off my orgasm and then Gray's.

My vision went dark for a second before I recovered.

Felix trembled a little as we slipped out of him, and then I let him fall forward onto Gray's chest. My thighs were burning, and I was starting to feel the sweat that had run down my back cooling down.

I removed Gray's condom and mine and tied them before disposing of them in the bathroom, where I also got a wet cloth to clean them both.

"I don't think I can ever move from here," Gray said.

Felix had his eyes closed as Gray ran his hands up

and down his back. "You won't hear any complaints from me."

I forced them to part so I could clean them up and then settled on the bed next to Gray with Felix between us.

"How about a short nap and then lunch?" I asked.

They both replied with an *uh-huh* as they fell asleep. I pulled a blanket over us and let sleep take me too.

My last thought was that I'd never been happier to have almost drowned.

17

GRAYSON

I CLOSED my eyes and tightened my arms around Ev's waist. The island was disappearing slowly behind us, and the breeze as we rode the ferry back to LA was warm on my face.

"What are you thinking about?" Ev asked.

"How different this ride is compared to my ride to the island. It was only a few days ago, but I feel like I'm a different person. And it's not just because of us. I was in desperate need to slow down and switch off. I didn't know how much I needed it until now," I said.

"You work too much. Felix missed you a lot. He always made excuses, and he knew your work was important to you, but I know he missed you."

"Just him?"

Ev turned around to face me. We were eye to eye, close enough our noses touched.

"No, not just him. I missed you too. You don't even know how much. So many times I wanted to reach out, but I didn't know how."

"I know, baby. I felt the same way. I'm so glad Felix brought us together," I said.

"Do you think we'd ever have gotten our heads out of our butts if it hadn't been for Felix?"

I kissed him gently, licking his top lip and pulling on his tongue as it met mine.

"I don't know. I'd like to think we would have, but the truth is I don't know. But there's no point in wondering what if, because we're here now. We have each other. All three of us."

"It's crazy, right? I never thought I'd be with two guys at the same time, and somehow it feels so right. I'm questioning all my previous relationships and wondering if they were always doomed to fail because they weren't enough for me," Ev said.

"Are *we* enough for you, Ev?" I asked.

He tightened his hold around me. "More than enough, Gray. You and Felix are everything."

"Ev. You're not afraid of the water anymore?"

We turned our heads to Felix, who was returning from the small cafe on the ferry with three coffees.

"Oh no, I'm not afraid. I'm terrified," Ev said.

"In case you haven't noticed, you're leaning against the railing and there's water on the other side.

How come you're not having a panic attack like last time?"

Ev laughed. "I'm actually leaning against my boyfriend, thank you very much. And I'm trying not to look at whatever's happening behind me."

"You mean *our* boyfriend," Felix said.

"Hey, there's enough Gray to go around," I said.

"We know," they both said, and then looked down at my crotch.

I groaned. "If I get an erection in front of people, I'm blaming you."

Felix gave us our coffees, and we went to sit at one of the tables on the deck.

We drank our coffee in silence, but after a while, I could tell there was a lot not being said.

"What's up? You both look like your coffee is extra bitter."

Felix didn't look up, so I put my hand on his chin to raise his head so I could see his eyes.

"I don't know what happens next. At the risk of sounding really needy, I've dreamed about dating both of you for years...I don't want to go home on my own," he said.

I held his hand. "You don't have to. I'd love it if you'd both come over to my place tonight. We'll be tired from the flight, so we can order dinner in, watch a movie, and chill."

"How big is your bed?" Ev asked.

I wiggled my eyebrows. "Big enough, baby. Big enough."

"Sold."

Felix's smile lit up his whole face.

"We still have a lot to figure out, but I want to spend as much time with you as possible."

Felix was still on break from school, but I knew Ev would want to get back to the store.

"How about tomorrow we have a chill breakfast, and then I'll take you back to Brooklyn? It'll give me a chance to check out the apartment and see how much work it needs before I can move in," I said.

"Are you serious?" Ev asked. "You really want to move to Brooklyn?"

"Baby, I'd move to Nova Scotia if that's where you were," I said.

"And how about your family?" Ev asked.

There was no point pretending it wouldn't be an issue. While they'd never had a problem with me being gay, they were very much all about appearances. Their only son dating two men was bound to raise a few brows.

I wasn't willing to give Ev and Felix up or choose between them, so my parents would need to accept it. Or if they didn't, I was prepared to step away from the company.

It was a thought that only weeks ago would have been unimaginable. The company was everything to me. But now, I wanted more, and I knew I deserved to be happy.

There would be other companies, other jobs, but there were only two men on the planet I couldn't live without.

"This conversation is getting too heavy. What I want to know is who's gonna fuck me later," I said.

Ev almost choked on his coffee.

"What? You know I'm a planner. I like to know these things."

Felix laughed.

Yep, we were going to be okay.

Best vacation ever.

Dear reader, I hope you enjoyed this short trip into the world of Room for 3, and meeting Felix, Ev and Gray.

Mal, Griff and Jake make a short appearance here. If you're curious to find out how their story started then you can read it in The Resort, Book 1 in the Room for 3 series.

The Resort is available on Amazon to buy or read for free with Kindle Unlimited.

Get The Resort here: bit.ly/RoomFor3Resort

The Resort started as a newsletter serial I offered to my subscribers. All it took was a photo shared by a reader and the world of Room for 3 was born.

The sequel to The Resort, The Island is currently being offered to my newsletter subscribers. To access The Island subscribe to my newsletter, bit.ly/AnaAshley.

BOOKS BY ANA ASHLEY

Single Dads of Stillwater

A spin off series from Chester Falls that can be read on its own. Each book features one or more single dads in this community of friends, family and found family. In this contemporary MM romance series you'll find heat, emotion and a guaranteed happy ever after.

Newcomer

Antagonist

Breakthrough

Heartstring

Datebook (Coming late 2023)

Finding You Series

A standalone series set across the Atlantic between New York and Portugal. Find your way home with this contemporary MM romance series with friends to lovers, star-crossed lovers and age gap with plenty of heat, feels and always a happy ever after.

Home Again

Together Again

Love Again

And for a special short story, Complete Again, plus bonus scenes, grab the Finding You boxset now.

Room for 3 series

This is a high heat MMM contemporary romance series set in an island resort.

The Resort

The Vacation (Free short story)

Chester Falls Series

From a Prince to a Happy Ever After for all, enjoy this small town MM romance series that's as sweet as they come, with plenty of heat, humor and everything in between.

How to Catch a Bookworm (Prequel short)

How to Catch a Prince

How to Catch a Rival

How to Catch a Bodyguard

How to Catch a Bachelor

How to Catch the Boss (a Christmas novella)

How to Catch a Biker

How to Catch a Vet

How to Catch a Happy Ever After

You can now have all the books in the series and the

prequel all in two boxsets.

Chester Falls Collection Volume I

Chester Falls Collection Volume II

Standalone books

Christmas Bubble: a low angst, standalone, Christmas novel featuring a petite but larger-than-life cheerleader, an older demisexual football coach and a winter cabin by the lake with only one bed. With cameos from Chester Falls and Stillwater.

Midnight Ash: a sweet Cinderella fairytale retelling with a sexy kinky twist on the side, and a cast who don't quite behave as you'd expect.

Stronghold: a sweet and sexy romance in Sarina Bowen's World of True North, Vino & Veritas series. This is a standalone story between two childhood friends who reunite after as decade apart, with some creative use of maple syrup.

FREE READS

My Fake Billionaire - Amazon

My Fake Billionaire - All stores

The Vacation (Free short story)

AUDIOBOOKS BY ANA ASHLEY

A lot of my books are now available on audiobook through Amazon/Audible and iTunes.

Dads of Stillwater narrated by John Solo

Newcomer

Antagonist

Breakthrough

Heartstring

Chester Falls narrated by Nick Hudson

How to Catch a Bookworm (a short prequel)

How to Catch a Prince

How to Catch a Rival

How to Catch a Bodyguard

How to Catch Bachelor

How to Catch the Boss (a Christmas novella)

How to Catch a Biker

How to Catch a Vet

How to Catch a Happy Ever After

Stronghold narrated by John Solo

ABOUT ANA

Ana Ashley was born in Portugal but has lived in the United Kingdom for so long, even her friends sometimes doubt if she really is Portuguese.

After getting hooked on reading gay romance, Ana decided to follow her lifelong dream of becoming an author.

These days you can find her in front of her laptop bringing her stories to life, or in the kitchen perfecting her recipe for the famous Portuguese custard tarts.

Ana Ashley writes sweet and steamy gay romance set in America, often in small towns where everyone knows everyone.

You can follow Ana on the usual social media hangouts.

For access to exclusive teasers, content, and general book and food related goodness you can now join Ana in her Facebook Group, Café RoMMance - Ana's Reader Group

Ana's VIP Readers - bit.ly/AnaAshley

Facebook Page - @anawritesmm

Email - ana@anaashley.com

Instagram - @anawritesmm

Bookbub - bookbub.com/authors/ana-ashley

Goodreads - goodreads.com/ana-ashley